Joe Hipp is a retired Air Force Navigator, studied Journalism at Texas A&M, landed a Texas Press Association internship on the San Antonio Express-News before graduation in 1954. That began his writing career. He flew in the backseat of an Air Defense Command F-89, running intercepts until released from active duty, worked on a weekly newspaper until recalled in 1959 (Lebanon Crisis). With tours in England, Vietnam and Germany, he retired from the Air Force in 1986, and began traveling in a motorhome, volunteering with Habitat for Humanity and church builders. Writing three non-fiction books and his first novel, he settled in the Army Residence Community. Traveling the Lewis and Clark trail several times, he discovered the story of 'Walks With Bear.'

To friends and family making their own Quest.

Joe Hipp

THE STORY OF WALKS WITH BEAR AND BRO'KEN

AUSTIN MACAULEY PUBLISHERS™

LONDON * CAMBRIDGE * NEW YORK * SHARJAH

This is a work of fiction. Names, characters, businesses, places, events, locales, and incidents are either the products of the author's imagination or used in a fictitious manner. Any resemblance to actual persons, living or dead, or actual events is purely coincidental.

Ordering Information
Quantity sales: Special discounts are available on quantity purchases by corporations, associations, and others. For details, contact the publisher at the address below.

Publisher's Cataloging-in-Publication data
Hipp, Joe
The Story of Walks with Bear and Bro'Ken

ISBN 9798891552814 (Paperback)
ISBN 9798891552821 (Hardback)
ISBN 9798891552838 (ePub e-book)

Library of Congress Control Number: 2024900373

www.austinmacauley.com/us

First Published 2024
Austin Macauley Publishers LLC
40 Wall Street, 33rd Floor, Suite 3302
New York, NY 10005
USA

mail-usa@austinmacauley.com
+1 (646) 5125767

John and Pat Seawell diligently read the draft manuscript and provided substantive changes. Susan Brown tackled the manuscript to make sure I got the story straight. Senior daughter, Denise ZitzEvancih, collected and organized research material to make it a better story. Both daughters, Denise and Carilyn, designed and created a cover for the book. Thanks to all of you!

First novel by Joe Hipp:
All in a Lifetime
The Story of Anya, Wilhelm, and an Icon

Prologue

"A man's heart devises his way, but God directs his steps." Those words are from Proverbs, chapter 16. A lot of good advice there. For you the reader, years ago my "heart's desire" was to follow the Lewis and Clark Trail in my Beaver Patriot motorhome during the period of "re-enactment". Aided by "The Journals of Lewis and Clark", the works of Stephen Ambrose and Bernard DeVoto, I traveled the Ohio, Mississippi, Missouri, and Columbia Rivers; from Pittsburg to Fort Clatsop, I looked for relevant untold stories, factual or fiction. Stumbling across stories I met several Ogala Sioux at a Black Hills Pow Wow, saw events, gathered family stories, and began writing. This is a work of fiction, meant to entertain and not detract from the monumental achievements of Captains Lewis and Clark on their journey to the Pacific.

To steal ideas from one person is plagiarism; to steal from many is research, and so goes the *Paraprosdokian* I use in describing Bro-Ken. *Paraprosdokians* (a Greek term) are figures of speech where the last part of a sentence (or phrase) "…is surprising or unexpected and is frequently humorous." The stories are from many heard in my travels and were not plagiarized, but rather researched. The storyteller is my fictional friend, Brother Ken, although there was a real "Brother Ken". The story of Walks-With-Bear is the antithesis to what most believe about the American Indian, and about some White captives that were repatriated.

Chapter One
The Obsidian Blade

These are stories told by Kentucky Baptiste Bellefleur, born in Spanish Sainte Louis, in January 1800, a storyteller and adventurer. His grandfather, Walks-With-Bear, introduced Kentucky to the art of storytelling. Kentucky was later known as Brother Ken, shortened to Bro-Ken, by members of his church.

My grandfather, a tall dark-skinned Shawnee named Kenthaki, was also called Walks-With-Bear for reasons you will discover. I called him Paw and he told me many stories, one I recall best is about a mysterious Obsidian knife passed down through time. I still have the knife. Growing up in what is now Ohio, the son of a Shawnee chief, he told me about going on his "Quest". Paw ended up in Missouri where I was born, listening to his stories, and starting my own story.

In his last days he said, *"Look to Heaven, that is where your Father is, regard Earth as a mother, and all the people you meet, they are your brothers and sisters."* It took me a while to understand his words of wisdom.

First, a story of the Obsidian Blade, starting before Paw was born. In the volcanic region of the Great Northwest, there was a massive eruption that killed many people dwelling on the slopes of a majestic cone-shaped mountain. This happened long before Meriwether Lewis and Thomas Clark ventured into the area, even before British and French explorers found the land of volcanoes. The people living there were the earliest explorers, perhaps crossing the land bridge from present-day Russia to Alaska. Driven south by the search for a better climate, or game, they reached the Columbia River Basin and lived on and near the mountains. There they could fish and hunt year around.

Early tribes were close to nature and after the eruption that killed so many, their wise men claimed the mountain spirit wanted a sacrifice, deciding a pure, young maiden would satisfy the mountain spirit. Selecting one and taking her to the edge of the caldera, two warriors lifted her and threw her into the molten lava bubbling below. The warriors were too close to the edge and when they threw her, the ground beneath their feet gave way and they too fell into the caldera.

For a while, it seemed the sacrifice satisfied the mountain spirit, but days later an eruption sent lava spewing into the air containing liquid glass, Obsidian. (**Obsidian**, dark, semi-translucent volcanic glass of the same composition as rhyolite, produced when molten igneous rock, magma, pushes its way up to the earth's surface and cools so rapidly that its constituent ions do not have time to crystallize.) As it cooled and solidified, the Indians ventured back to the mountain. They examined the Obsidian and a red steak appeared in some of the broken pieces of the otherwise black material. "The blood of the sacrifice," the wise men declared.

A century passed and the mountain remained dormant. The sacrifice was not forgotten. Tribes in the area collected the Obsidian and traded it to other tribes for fashioning spearheads, arrowheads, and knife blades. Obsidian found with traces of the blood sacrifice was treasured. Properly knapped, the Obsidian became the sharpest blade a warrior could have. *Obsidian blades are among the sharpest, if not the sharpest, blades known to man. Surgeons have been known to prefer an obsidian blade since it reduces scar tissue.*

In the late 1600s, a Nez Perce Indian recovered a slab of Obsidian found on the slopes of "Glass Mountain" in the high desert of present-day Oregon. He traded it to a Blackfoot warrior during their summer trading time in the land of present-day Montana. The warrior's sister, a Blackfoot maiden, was a skilled "flint-knapper"; knapping is the process of chipping away at stone, flint, or Obsidian, to make a useful object. As she traveled east with her brother and a small band of Blackfoot warriors, she worked, chipping away at the edges of the Obsidian as they traveled, hunting and exploring toward the land of Big Lakes. While "knapping" the edges of the obsidian, the interior of the slab changed color and became translucent. The more she knapped to form a knife blade; a crimson streak began to appear in the heart of the now translucent Obsidian. She chipped around it to reveal a crimson shape looking like a dagger, or a cross encased in the translucent Obsidian. Not knowing the history of the 'sacrifice', but aware that her knapping had revealed something unusual, she was reluctant to share her discovery with others in the small band of Blackfeet.

It was after the turn of the century, 1700 when the Blackfeet met a similarly small band of Shawnee hunters and explorers. They shared stories of their adventure, exploits, and home ground. A Shawnee warrior admired the beauty and industry of the Blackfoot maiden and asked her brother if he could take the maiden as his squaw. The Shawnee and the maiden had "chemistry." How that arrangement was worked out is unclear, perhaps some bartering, or bloodletting (becoming blood brothers). Regardless, an arrangement was made, and the Blackfoot maiden became a Shawnee squaw of the Water Panther Clan. The deal was sealed when the Blackfoot maiden gave Shawnee warrior a knife blade made of Obsidian, mounted in a haft of elkhorn, *wapiti*. That union, or marriage, and the Obsidian blade became part of the legend of "Walks with a Bear."

Chapter Two
Ken-tha-ki (or, Walks
With-Bear)

The Shawnee warrior with a Blackfoot squaw became a leader in his clan. In the course of time, he became their Chief and acquired Shawnee squaws; chiefs often had several squaws to maintain their expanding "household". His Shawnee name became "Chief Many Squaws". When the Blackfoot Squaw bore him a son, two elder members of the clan were chosen to seek a name. In a vision, they saw living, dancing waters. Ken-tha-ki is a Shawnee term for the source of living water and was the name offered to Paw's father and his squaw. It is also said to be the origin of the name given to the state of Kentucky.

So, Paw was named Kenthaki. When he was 15 winters old, his father gave him a knife (the one with the Obsidian blade knapped by his Nez Perce squaw), a flint scraping tool used to prepare pelts, some powerful medicine from his cache (a personal pharmacopeia) and sent him on a quest. Paw had been told of earlier adventures to the land of Big Lakes by members of the tribe, which would be his destination. In his pouch, Paw carried the scraping tool and a drinking shell along with 'medicine', herbs, and roots.

Leaving the village of Tshilikauthee (pronounced Che-le-co-the) in early summer, he traveled north through dense forests of hickory, oak, and walnut trees, to the Big Lake on the northern border of present-day Ohio. It is a Shawnee belief that during such a quest, challenges, or a challenge, will arise and make the quest memorable. He fastened the knife to an eight-foot Hickory pole; it became a spear for extending the range of use. In the forest near the Big Lakes, a giant black bear was feeding. Observing the bear for a while, it seemed content and harmless. A sound must have startled the bear for it suddenly rose up from feeding, looked in Paw's direction, roared, and charged. Using his spear to keep a distance, he placed several deep jabs into its neck and heart. It eventually fell and bled out on the torn-up ground where they had fought. Paw was not without his own wounds; the claws of the bear had reached his arms and legs. Using powerful medicine from his pouch, he wrapped his wounds using Catawba leaves and leather thongs.

Paw had never seen a bear this size in all of his 15 winters. The fight exhausted him. He sat beside the bear to figure out what to do with the skin and meat the bear would provide. Skinning the bear was the first challenge. Unable to hoist the dead bear upon a tree limb, it was heavy, he cleared an area around the bear and, making a bed of leaves and branches, rolled the carcass onto the cleared area. There he skinned the bear, keeping the head attached to the hide and removing the edible meat. Using his flint scraping tool, he cleaned the hide and proceeded to apply a curing potion known to Indians, Paw never told me what it was. A small male cub wandered up, sniffed, and lay down nearby. It was then Paw realized the bear was a sow (female), little wonder it had fought so fiercely. There is a saying: "Don't mess with a mother bear."

Slicing long strips of meat from the shoulders of the bear, he cooked some for his own use and smoked and jerked the rest for the return journey. After scraping and drying the bear skin, a task taking several days, he rolled it up. Cutting a large slab of bark from a tree and making a sled, he rigged a harness and, with the bear cub close at his heels, departed for Tshilikauthee.

The cub knew the smell of its mother and followed. Blackberries were ripening and plentiful in the forest. While Paw ate a handful of berries, the cub approached and sniffed the pelt and the berries. Paw held out a piece of bark with berries on it. The cub took the berries in one quick lap of its tongue. It was the beginning of a long journey for Kenthaki and Makwa (Shawnee for bear).

On returning to the village Paw gained another name, Tecumakwa, meaning "Walks with a Bear". It was not common to have bears in the village, other wild animals perhaps, but not large bears. The senior squaw insisted he keeps the bear (Makwa) caged while in the village.

* * *

Far to the southeast of Tshilikauthee (Chillicothe) an event was happening that would greatly influence the life of Tecumakwa. A German farming community (*started by John Jacob Riemensperger immigrant agent, in South*

Carolina's 'back country', ceded from Cherokee Indians), had just ended their Sunday services and Stefan Boucher herded his family to their wagon for the short journey home. Elizabeth, his youngest daughter, asked to stay and picnic with friends who would deliver her home after the picnic. It was a frequent request for the popular and fun-loving 'Lizabeth', and was quickly granted by Papa Stefan.

Shortly after the adults left a group of Indians approached. The young people were not frightened for Indians had befriended many of the German families. Quite often, they would ask for any remaining food from their picnic and be on their way. Elizabeth noticed the braves were different from those she was accustomed to seeing, their faces were painted and they carried weapons. She urged her friends to move toward the church. Before they could reach the safety of the church doors, the young Germans were surrounded, captured, secured, and began a long journey north to be sold as slaves.

* * *

In Tshilikauthee a raiding party returned from the south with a young girl captive. She was given to Chief Many Squaws to help in his lodge. (*Southern Shawnees often made exchanges with Cherokees in South Carolina. German settlers were given grants of land by the British in what was considered Cherokee lands. Cherokees raided the German settlements, capturing their own slave labor to be sent north.*) Her name was **Elizabeth Boucher** and her parents, not among the captives, were German immigrants. Two winters passed and Elizabeth was like a sister to Kenthaki. She taught him English using a bible she had in her apron when captured. Kenthaki taught her their sign language and some Shawnee words. At first, she was afraid of Makwa. But, after a few visits, her presence was accepted by Makwa, and she tolerated Makwa.

Kenthaki learned about her God being a peaceful God, a God for all people, perhaps her God was *Moneto,* God of the universe (or, the Great Spirit, Master of life). The Bible, and Elizabeth, taught Kenthaki a different way of life, to love all people. The first words she taught were from the book of John. Paw managed to write the words on the tablet paper Elizabeth had found. He folded it and placed it in his pouch along with the scraping tool, drinking shell, and medicines for wounds.

Living near the Ohio River, Paw saw many white people rafting downstream. As long as they remained on their side of the river, the Shawnee accepted their use of the river and the brief stops made on the Shawnee side to visit and trade. There were treaties allowing them to pass through tribal lands, and have prisoner exchanges with white settlers. In one of those exchanges, Elizabeth was allowed to leave. She gave Paw her English bible as she prepared to go, with a personal note written and placed inside. In the note, she called him her Indian brother. Returning to what is now South Carolina, Elizabeth Boucher became a teacher, married, and had children. She is buried in Hurricane Baptist Church Cemetery, her grave marked by a simple stone, "*Elizabeth*".

In 1766, an American geographer, Thomas Hutchins, came drifting down the Ohio River with a party, led by Indian trader George Crogan. There were Shawnee and Delaware in the party, to maintain a peaceful journey. News of their coming reached all villages and Kenthaki watched from the north bank as they drifted by. They began their journey at Fort Pitt and continued down the Ohio all the way to the Mississippi River. Some settlers followed them; one Kenthaki eventually met. A retired British officer, Reginald Foote, tagged along to find a place to settle his family among peaceful Indians in the west. His claim of land near the junction of the Wabash and Ohio Rivers was officially recorded by the British governor of the Western Provinces.

As years passed frontier white men called him the tall Indian, with a nose like an eagle's beak, he walks with a bear, Tecumakwa among the Shawnee, and "Walks-With-Bear" by the colonials. He walked the Ohio forests cradling an English-made flintlock rifle and "Makwa," by then a mature black bear, was always at his side. At this time Shawnee warriors were among the most feared of the eastern Indian tribes. Kenthaki's new beliefs from his "Bible" that we should love all mankind puzzled those in the village. How can we love all men when they take our land?

There was reason to walk the forests with caution in 1774, but 20-year-old Kenthaki "Tecumakwa", walked without fear. The British and colonists were not happy with each other, and the French and Indians were not happy with either the British or the colonists. Other than his rifle and drinking shell, he carried three items of personal value: a medicine pouch to heal maladies and wounds; a bag of selected planting seeds, including corn, squash, and others without a name; and his father's long-bladed knife of Obsidian, once again mounted in a well-worn haft of elk antler. And, of course, Makwa was by his side.

Meanwhile, agreements between Indian chiefs and the British had been broken. The westward migration into Indian hunting grounds was too widespread and difficult for Lord Dunmore, Governor of Virginia, to halt. Talks to resolve issues had failed and Shawnee Chief Cornstalk called for warrior volunteers to turn back the flood of settlers entering their lands from Virginia. The anger of the Indians turned into bloody warfare in early 1774 when a group of settlers murdered the entire family of Logan, a friendly Mingo chief. According to historians, "In September 1774, Dunmore signed peace treaties with Delaware and Six Nations of the Iroquois at Pittsburg. He then started down the Ohio River to give battle to the fierce Shawnee." The Shawnee had aligned themselves with Logan's Mingos.

Paw joined other Shawnee warriors at Point Pleasant, called "tu-endie-wei," by the Wyandottes, "the point between two waters." The Ohio and Kanawha rivers converge at that spot. A memorial of that battle, October 10, 1774, still stands at Point Pleasant, an 84-foot granite obelisk. Several chiefs united under Chief Cornstalk to stop the British immigrant invasion. Aging 'Chief Many Squaws' stayed behind. During the day-long battle "Makwa" frequently surprised and routed British patrols as they approached.

The initial charge by British forces was led by Colonel Charles Lewis of the Agusta County Regiment. He was mortally wounded. During the battle, a backwoodsman, fighting with the British, loaded and primed two muskets, one to kill the bear, the other to kill the Indian. Kenthaki knew they were being stalked by a red-haired backwoodsman, and saw glimpses of him. When the stalker spotted Kenthaki in an exposed position, he raised his musket and fired. But "Makwa" chose that moment to rise up from his grazing and took the full force of the shot to his left foreleg, near the paw. He might have heard the soldier's approach, or hasty move to shoot, but he saved Paw's life. The backwoodsman was unable to take his second shot and fled leaving Paw to tend to "Makwa", who was roaring in pain. As Makwa's pain subsided, Paw examined the wound and was able to remove the lead shot that had pierced his skin. He wrapped the bear's leg with leaves and medicine and secured the bandage with strips of leather.

As the Shawnee left the battlefield that evening in 1774 and crossed the Ohio River, Paw resolved to find the white man with red hair who wounded

"Makwa". Perhaps then he could make peace with white men and stop shedding blood. One chief who did not survive was Pucksinwah (or Puckeshinwau), the father of Tecumseh. He too was mortally wounded on the battlefield and carried back to Ohio. The British and backwoodsmen had prevailed, 230 Indians were killed or wounded and over 50 Virginians were killed.

After the battle, Paw began to see white men everywhere along the Ohio River. In his village, a few braves wanted to carry the fight to the white man, set traps for them, and destroy their rafts on the river. The memory of his "white sister", Elizabeth, had him on the opposite side of the fight. Living in peace with the white man became a goal; he had changed.

When Chief Many Squaws went to the "Happy Hunting Grounds", his leadership could have passed to his eldest son, Kenthaki. But tribal leaders decided on another leader for the "Water Panther Clan", one who would lead them into battle.

Chapter Three
A New Quest

With "Makwa" following, Paw departed the Shawnee village on a spring morning following a trail along the north bank of the Ohio westward, crossing the Wabash River into what is now Illinois. After traveling for several days, he met an Englishman, a retired British officer, at the juncture of a creek and the Ohio River, called "Foote's Landing". Foote had served under Sir William Johnson, an Irishman, First Baronet of New York, British Army, and a romantic attachment to a Mohawk maiden named Molly (or Mary) Brant. Siding with the British, she used her influence as a consort to Sir William to foment trouble between the colonists and Indian nations. Foote wanted no part of the conflict and headed West to lay claim to a plot of land west of where the Wabash River flows into the Ohio, a claim granted him earlier by the Governor of Western Provinces.

Reginald Foote was waiting for a supply boat from Kentucky and welcomed Paw to rest with him. Surprised at Paw's ability to speak English, and more impressed by the black bear that followed him, Foote asked if he would like a job working on his farm. Paw's response was cautious, "May I see your 'council house?'"

After the supply boat arrived, Kenthaki and Makwa assisted Colonel Foote in loading a wheelbarrow with supplies for the journey to his home (council house). A rope harness was secured to Makwa and attached to the barrow. The house was situated on high ground with land cleared on all sides for farming. Colonel Foote's family consisted of a wife, two sons, and three daughters. They were all on the porch of the house watching the procession approached, the Colonel steering his wheelbarrow, pulled by a large bear, being led by a tall Indian. The smaller children hid behind the skirts of the mother while the older son and daughter watched in stunned surprise as Kenthaki, and Makwa came toward them.

Following introductions, and the opportunity for Kenthaki to survey the area, he agreed to stay and help with the farming in return for a personal shelter and plot of land to work as his own. The Colonel allotted Kenthaki un-cleared land near the river and close to Foote's Landing. Paw set about clearing his land and building his own "council house". He rigged a harness for Makwa and, with some coaxing, Makwa was pulling stumps from the land and dragging logs to build the "council house."

There was a village nearby called Shawnee Town, started by Pekowi Shawnee, and Peter Chartier. It was known as a safe anchorage for rafts on the Ohio. Colonel Foote had met him on his voyage down the Ohio, following Geographer Thomas Hutchins in 1766. During the Revolutionary War, Shawnees sided with the British. Colonel Foote found acceptance with Shawnee Indians and lived in peace among them.

Establishing himself, Paw started another Shawnee village in 1782 in Southern Illinois, near Foote's Landing, as others from his tribe drifted westward, finding shelter and food at "Kenthaki's" council house. If they were peaceful, Colonel Foote was content to have help with his growing farmland and enterprises. Paw began dressing like the white man, wearing a broad-brimmed hat, jacket, and trousers, while ensuring his "settlers" were peaceful. The variety of Indian tribes passing through Kenthaki's settlement grew as White Settlers moved west. Most of the travelers who stopped over, refreshed, at his settlement were surprised a Shawnee could live peacefully with Englishmen, Frenchmen, Spaniards, and members of other tribes. Even more astonishing, black families found a haven at Paw's growing settlement. They grew accustomed to a large black bear following the leader of the settlement until one day the bear left the area and never returned.

Paw was tall, about six-foot-two, and literate. He even adapted to using an Englishman's pipe to smoke the tobacco they grew. It was readily apparent that Kenthaki impressed Marjorie Foote, the oldest daughter of Colonel Foote. She found excuses to visit Kenthaki, carry him water as he worked in the fields, and take him food at the end of the day. She was tall with blonde hair, fair-skinned and buxom.

Colonel Foote, following a custom of many who had slaves or sharecroppers, offered Paw his last name. Paw said, "I thought about it for a while and decided not to be called, 'Walks with Bear (bare) Foote'. The Colonel accepted my decision with a chuckle."

When Missionary Jedediah Mason arrived in the area and started a small congregation near the village (comprised of immigrant farmers, French-Canadian trappers, escaped slaves, and Shawnees), the inevitable happened, nothing apocalyptic. The Colonel's family attended the services, along with Kenthaki who remembered the "teaching" of his "white sister", Elizabeth. When Reverend Mason preached about love and marriage, the seed was planted. Paw's reluctance to marry outside his "tribe" was overcome. The strong feelings he had for Marjorie Foote, and her admiration of the Indian who walked with a bear, had helped her family and led an exemplary life, meshed. They fell in love, and, in due course, the couple asked Reverend Mason to marry them over the strenuous objections of Colonel Foote.

They were married in 1779, and a daughter, Hua-Neeta, was born in 1780. Disowned, but not dismissed, the newlyweds continued to live on Colonel Foote's property in Kenthaki's Council House. Another of Colonel Foote's daughters married a *Métis* (the name applied to anyone with mixed Indian and European ancestry) named Swader and settled nearby.

About that time a French-Canadian trapper, Jean Baptiste Bellefleur (Pretty Flower), became a frequent visitor at the Shawnee Town trading post. Bellefleur's ancestry, as he was told by his father, came from a mixture of Viking and Norman-French blood. *In the year 1000 as Vikings became frequent visitors to the waters of the English Channel, a Viking named Olaf Balfor met a French lass, became a Christian, and married her. Their offspring included a son who sailed with other Vikings to a new land, later named Iceland. From there he joined an expedition going farther west, beyond Greenland to explore a land inhabited by North American Indians, later called Canada. In the voyage and journey inland, the descendant of Olaf Balfor changed his name to a more European/French nom de plume, Bellefleur. And, from that lineage came Jean Baptiste Bellefleur, a mixture of Viking, French, Indian, and Norman intermarriage.*

Bellefleur could speak several languages, French, English, and Iroquois (including their sign language). He had met, traveled, and trapped in Canada with Francois Verendrye, son of the famed French explorer. George Droulliard (also called Drewyer), a French-Canadian with a Shawnee mother, spoke French, English, and Shawnee. The two men had trapped the Wabash for several years with a base camp near the Ohio rapids at Louisville. On one of their trips, a red-haired frontiersman from Louisville accompanied Bellefleur and Droulliard. When they stopped at the landing near Kenthaki's settlement a meeting took place with strange overtones.

Kenthaki remembered the red-haired man who had shot Makwa and, although time had diminished his memory, the man's size and stature looked the same. Approaching the trio, Kenthaki raised his hand in greeting and asked if the red-haired man was at the Point Pleasant battle. The man was surprised and admitted he knew of the battle from what his father had told him, his father also had red hair. "Did he tell you of an Indian with a bear?" It slowly dawned on the redhead that maybe it was his father who had that encounter. The two men sat and talked, Thomas Clark of his father and Kenthaki of Makwa. They shared jerky Maw brought them and parted, peacefully. Kenthaki's transition from warrior to "man of peace" was complete. The influence of a young female captive on the life of a Shawnee warrior had remarkable results.

Chapter Four
My Parents

Jean Baptiste met *"la belle vertueux"*, Hua-Neeta, at the Shawnee Town Trading Post in 1798. He followed her everywhere when not trapping, made a pest of himself, even helping Kenthaki with some farm chores to be near her. He followed her to church not realizing how long Jedediah Mason preached and the interest he, an apparent Frenchman, would attract from the congregation. A part-time Catholic, he would do anything to spend more time with the "prettiest girl around."

They were married by Preacher Mason in 1799, and Jean Baptiste had to get busy supporting a wife. A Spanish fur trader in Saint Louis, Manuel Lisa, offered him a job examining pelts in his shop. Moving to Saint Louis in 1800, a son, Kentucky Baptiste Bellefleur, was born that year to the French-Canadian, and *Métis* (Hua-Neeta), in Spanish-owned Saint Louis. Saint Louis was still a young town, having been established in 1764 as a center of fur trading by Pierre Laclede Liguest. Auguste Chouteau said to be his common-law stepson, was put in charge of clearing the land. From old records, we found a quote: "You will proceed and land at a place where we marked the trees; you will commence to clear the place and build a large shed to contain the provisions and tools, then build some small cabins to lodge the men." Laclede later visited the site, laid out a plan for the village, selected a site for his house to be built, and left. That is how it started.

In the first years of their marriage, Hua-Neeta was not idle. She made a variety of objects from pieces of fur Jean Baptiste brought her. The city life was exciting, Spanish troops paraded frequently along the city streets, and sailing boats offloaded visitors from other countries. Her firstborn was a happy child, easy to manage, and behaved well with strangers. This allowed Hua-Neeta to travel across the river to Cahokia and sell her wares. On one of those trips in 1802, while the river was nearing flood stage, the boat she was in capsized, striking a drifting log. Her long black hair became entangled in a snag, and as the boatman struggled to save the boat, she was pulled beneath the water. Hua-Neeta disappeared in the swift flowing muddy water of the Mississippi River, never to be seen again.

A message from Jean Baptiste to Kenthaki and Marjorie brought them swiftly to Saint Louis to care for their grandson. It was an easy decision for them. A Shawnee warrior named Tecumseh was stirring up trouble against white men in Ohio and Indiana. Peaceful settlers in Illinois territory feared the trouble would reach them and many living near Kenthaki's council house began moving further west. Colonel Foote found a black family eager to establish their own place in the Shawnee village and allowed them to use the land as 'sharecroppers'.

Settling first in the Bellefleur house, Kenthaki and Marjorie decided to find a farm outside the bustling city. With money saved, and help from Jean Baptiste, they bought a farm north of the city near the Missouri River and a lake. Jean Baptiste, Kentucky, Kenthaki, and Marjorie, became a family in the expanding rural area around Saint Louis and Paw could use his skills farming and hunting in peace. That area, where I grew up, would become known as 'Bellefontaine-Spanish Lake'.

The year 1803, brought many changes. Spain had given their territory in America to the French, on October 1, 1800, in the treaty of Ildefonso. Spain was not eager to turn over its' last footprint on American soil and it was not until July 1802, that Spanish officials were finally told to deliver possession of the land to French officials. On December 20, 1803, in New Orleans, William Claiborne, and General James Wilkinson, representing the United States, accepted the transfer of 800,000 square miles of land from French authorities. The flag of Spain still flew over Saint Louis.

France had already sold their combined territories, the Port of New Orleans and Louisiana, to President Thomas Jefferson, known as the Louisiana Purchase, on April 30, 1803. A short time later, President Jefferson commissioned his aide, Meriwether Lewis, to take a voyage of discovery into this new territory now owned by the United States. To clarify a point, Spanish soldiers were still in charge at Saint Louis until that December. Word about the transfer of ownership had perhaps deliberately traveled slowly! Captain

Lewis authorized the construction of a Keelboat near Pittsburg on the Ohio River, then started his journey to the west, along with two pirogues.

In November 1803, the Corps of Discovery stopped at Shawnee Town, looking for a guide and hunter for their expedition. They needed more men to round out the team and found George Drouillard at Fort Massac hiring him as a civilian member of the Corps of Discovery, to hunt, interpret, and scout. Drouillard recommended Jean Baptiste as another civilian hunter, but Jean Baptiste had left the area. The Corps picked up several more military members for the journey while at Fort Massac. After Fort Massac, the adventurers made winter camp across the Mississippi from Saint Louis, north of Cahokia at the mouth of Wood River.

Re-enactment Photo

An Artists Version

It was not until the spring of 1804, that Spanish authorities in Saint Louis finally gave control of the upper part of the Louisiana Purchase to Captain Amos Stoddard, the U.S. Army, and the Corps of Discovery could depart from their camp on the Wood River. After searching, George Droulliard found Jean Baptiste in Saint Louis and asked if he would follow along as an unofficial hunter/provider for the first part of a great journey up the Missouri. Manuel Lisa quickly realized the opportunities for his fur business and encouraged Jean Baptiste to make the journey, offering to pay his way. So, with provisions provided by Lisa, and a promise from Thomas Clark to compensate him on their return, Jean Baptiste departed with the Corps of Discovery and never returned. What happened to him is another story. Much was happening in Saint Louis at the time, most residents were French, and Manuel Lisa was Spanish. The uniqueness of Senor Lisa cannot be ignored.

Lisa arrived in Saint Louis from New Orleans in 1796 and began trading in furs small time. When the Lewis and Clark expedition returned safely, Lisa and a group of trappers paddled west on the Missouri and returned the next year loaded down with furs. He was known to the Indians as a 'fair' trader and did some honest and not-so-profitable trading to establish himself. His efforts in the fur trading business earned him a living, but he did not become rich.

* * *

Thomas Clark about Jean Baptiste Bellefleur

On our return trip in August of 1806, we visited the lodge of a Cheyenne Chief in the vicinity of where we had last seen the hunter, Jean Baptiste Bellefleur. It had been a long day, we smoked a few "pipes" and that evening I asked if he had seen our missing hunter. It had been reported to him a group of Cheyennes adopted a Frenchman, a skilled hunter, and trapper, and moved farther west toward the great mountains. That was all he knew.

* * *

When it was apparent Jean Baptiste had been separated from the expedition (near present-day Atchison, Kansas) and was not returning, Manuel Lisa offered to provide Kentucky with an education in a school he owned in Saint Louis. Thomas Clark had arranged for the son of Sacajawea and Touissant

Charbonneau to attend the same school. Manuel Lisa, still hoping to capitalize on the expedition, employed George Drouillard to return and establish a trading post near the Yellowstone Country. In accepting the job, Drouillard hoped to find some trace of his missing friend, Bellefleur. It was there in the Yellowstone Country Drouillard met his death in 1810, mutilated by the Indians he was trying to benefit. So was lost any hope of finding Jean Baptiste.

Maw and Paw raised Kentucky as their own, home-schooled by Maw. They accepted Mr. Lisa's offer and enrolled him in the Saint Louis school, a fortuitous move. It was a good school, Lisa had hired the best teachers he could find, and there he met Jean Baptiste Charbonneau; they became friends. Charbonneau had a nickname, "Pompey" – meaning Little Chief in the Shoshoni language. Kentucky was 11 years old, Jean Baptiste was 7 years old. Between going to school in Saint Louis and spending time with Maw and Paw at their farm, Kentucky learned to use a bow and arrow, fire a rifle, skin and dress a rabbit and attended their church north of Saint Louis in the Bellefontaine-Spanish Lake area where he became a Christian. He also acquired a brother named James, an orphaned black youth Maw and Paw adopted. James was younger and easily frightened by Kentucky's friends. Kentucky was his protector.

In Mr. Lisa's school, Kentucky learned to read and write French and Greek, along with English. That first year in school was memorable; in spring there was a big flood, between the bluffs on each side of the river there was nothing but water, and in December 1811, a great earthquake shook the town; tremors rattled the Mississippi Valley. Mr. Lisa let Kentucky stay in town. The school was closed for a week. When Kentucky brought books home, he let James look at them and Maw would teach him words and explain the stories. She treated him the same as she treated Kentucky.

When Kentucky learned a "Juvenile Company" was being formed, an infantry company of "young men between 14 and 18 years of age, to do duty when called upon, south of the Missouri River" he talked Paw into letting him volunteer. They lived in an area needing to be defended from marauding Indians who would nocturnally slip down from north of the Missouri River and take livestock, and/or pillage the locals. Kentucky became a member of the "Juvenile Company". He also began keeping a journal, perhaps influenced by the Journals of Lewis and Clark.

In the church they attended, descendants of Spanish, French, and Indian settlers were congregants. A Spanish lady painted a portrait of Paw and gave it to him as a gift.

Kenthaki in his 70s

Paw was well-liked by the Bellefontaine community and even made a deacon in the church. In the spring of 1817, Maw and Paw fell ill, and many neighbors and church members succumbed to a Cholera epidemic. Paw had ministered to the sick with his native remedies and contracted the disease. There were no doctors outside Saint Louis, at that time. They died a slow, treatable death. In 1854, Dr. John Snow in England discovered the cause of

Cholera, it was transmitted through water they drank from contaminated water sources.

I was orphaned again, as was James. Members of the church wanted to adopt us and offered to help settle "the estate," such as it was. We were cared for by members of the church, that's how things worked and stayed in the home Maw and Paw built until it was sold. When James found a home with a black family, friends of Maw and Paw, I began making plans to depart Saint Louis. My long-planned 'quest' to find my father had arrived, and I now had the money to do so. The time had come.

Chapter Five
Kentucky's Story

Saint Louis

Summer 1817

Paw had told me stories from his past and said each story, if it was a good story, had another story hidden within. The story of the Obsidian Blade was part of another story about an Indian maiden offered as a sacrifice to the "Gods of the Volcano". The journey of the block of obsidian into the hands of his mother, "Blackfoot Squaw", is another story, and so it goes, stories within a story. Paw also told me of my own ancestry, a story he probably embellished to improve my self-image.

This is my story, Kentucky Baptiste Bellefleur, son of a missing French-Canadian (descended from Vikings) Jean Baptist Bellefleur, and Hua-Neeta Bellefleur, deceased wife of Bellefleur. In the church I attended with my grandparents, before their passing, the men were all called "Brother." The boys were called "Bro." My name was shortened to Bro Ken and that is a story for another time. My adopted brother was called Bro James.

To any observer along the streets of Saint Louis, I was just a tall, slightly built, sandy-haired young man with a pack over his shoulders, leaving town. Carrying Paw's old, long-barreled muzzle-loader, I was hurrying to escape the dust of the city and get on with my own 'quest'. Crossing town on foot presented problems. The streets were fortunately dry, unfortunately dusty, and wagons pulled by six-horse teams, carriages of every shape and size, and men and women on horseback stirred up the dust laying like a low cloud.

Making my way through the streets that paralleled the river, I carried a lot of memories in my pack. Resting on top was Paw's Bible, the one he received from his white "sister". Nestled beneath was a bag of seeds, Paw's obsidian knife, a flint scraping tool, some medicinal herbs Paw had given me, my journal, and a notebook for writing about my adventure. Hanging from my waist was an extra pair of shoes, hand-made by Paw from deer skin, a bed roll, and other things to help me on my journey (quest). Dust obscured the sadness in my face, hiding a tear, and perhaps that is why I stumbled in front of a wagon being led by the Reverend Jedediah Mason.

The Reverend and his family were heading down the Great Southwest Trail to establish a mission with the Cherokee Indians in Arkansas. They had completed a crossing of the river, two days earlier, and stayed with the pastor of a Baptist church being built of brick before continuing their journey. Wife Susannah, two daughters, and a son made up the party. His work in Ohio resulted in an established church and missionary-minded Jedediah was off in search of another "mission field". It is no coincidence the Reverend bumped into me, the Lord planned it. Mason had performed the marriage ceremony of my parents, Jean Baptiste Bellefleur and Hua-Neeta Foote in 1798, at a place called Shawnee Town. It was destined we should meet and start a journey together.

Recovering from my mishap, and after apologies and introductions, I joined the Mason family departing Saint Louis "headin' down the Great Southwest Trail," or Military Road as it was sometimes called. Making camp that evening after crossing a small stream south of the town, I used Paw's knife to clear the campsite. Reverend Mason's inquisitive children wanted to know more about the strange-looking knife. I told them to wait until our campsite was prepared for the night. After we had shared a meal and the campfire was burning, I told them what I knew of the "Obsidian Blade" and the mysterious coloring in its center. As the fire died down, I curled up against a log, near the Mason's wagon, said a prayer of thanks and fell asleep. It had been a comfortable start to my journey.

Travelers on the trail had left many signs of having been there. Teams of horses and oxen had traversed the trail hauling lead from the French mines southwest of the trail. The trail we followed was primarily for those traveling to Mexico and Texas. Reverend Mason was going to preach to the Cherokee Indians who had settled peacefully west of the Mississippi River, close to the Osage, a dominant tribe in Southwest Missouri and the Ozarks. Years later migrating Cherokees forced to leave their homelands in Eastern states, would follow some of the many signs left by early travelers on what became known as the "Trail of Tears." Reverend Mason was accustomed to preaching to

Indians of several tribes, most recently the Shawnee. He spoke several Indian languages and could "sign". That he had known my parents and my grandparents was a gift, a blessing.

A week into our journey we were beyond Cape Girardeau, leaving the Mississippi River behind. As we traveled down the trail, Reverend Mason told me stories of Shawnee Town, what a good man my grandfather was, how he treated people equally, and that Paw was the first Indian convert to join the church at Shawnee Town. At campfires along the trail, I listened while he wove stories about Indians and White Men co-existing and sharing religious beliefs. Each campsite revealed items left behind by other travelers. People were deciding what they really needed.

At a slow pace, through thick forests and cane brakes, it took several weeks to reach the Current River crossing at Hick's Ferry. There I began to collect castaway items for future use, a powder horn cracked but easily patched, and a metal boot lathe that had fallen into the muddy water along the bank. I figured a boot maker in the wilderness could earn a living repairing and making new footwear, particularly when raw materials were free, or easily bartered.

Ferry operators sometimes charged inordinately high fees to unsuspecting travelers, particularly those with a sign of wealth. By splitting up a party, he would leave the weakest of the party stranded until more money, or possessions, were transferred, usually at the end of the day complaining that an additional trip would cost him (the ferry operator) more in labor. Paw had told me of the trickery used by ferry operators on the Mississippi and Missouri rivers to split up travelers.

When the Hick's Ferry operator told Reverend Mason we had to split our party because he already had part of a load, I told Reverend Mason, "Tell him we'll wait until we can all board the same time!" It worked; he squeezed us onto the last load for the day and we camped near the landing. During the night we heard gunfire from the opposite side of the river, I was glad we had already crossed. The next day we continued down the trail toward the Arkansas River, our destination.

My English grandmother had taught me to address others formally, I called the Reverend's wife Miz Susannah and the oldest daughter Miss Sue. We had not gotten beyond that point in our relationship. When needed, I stood guard while the women bathed or did other chores that took them away from camp.

We had other rivers to cross before reaching the White River, called *La Rievere Blanche* by early French explorers.

Making camp for the weekend near the White River I killed a bear. It was Sunday afternoon and Reverend Jedediah had finished his bible reading and preaching for the time being. Miss Sue and the other children wandered toward the river looking for a place to wash dishes. In a canebrake by a creek, they found what they were looking for, but also found a bear foraging for berries, not looking for trouble. As was my custom I had followed them protectively with musket in hand. They saw the bear and screamed. Approaching the girls cautiously, I told them softly; "Be calm, stand still, don't run," which is exactly what they did not do. They ran screaming toward our camp. The bear charged after them, and I waited until I had a headshot. My aim was a little off, but I must have struck a blood vessel leading to the brain for the bear stopped, turned toward me, then fell.

Some nearby hunters heard my shot and came crashing through the canebrake. Seeing the bear dead on the ground, they asked what I planned to do with it. I told them, "Probably skin it and make some jerky from the meat." They offered jerky and some already cured bear meat if I would let them have the bear, while I wavered, they added to the offer, some gunpowder and shot, and transport across the river the next day. Reverend Mason approached us and, with his ecclesiastical presence, we reached an agreement that included some cash. These men extract oil from the bear's carcass and ship it downstream in troughs made of tree trunks. That is how the village of Oil Trough, Arkansas, was named.

The Southwest Trail crossed the White River at Poke (or Polk) Bayou. That is where we camped for a spell. Reverend Mason had heard of a trail from Poke Bayou to the Cherokee lands, due west. However, the safest route was to continue down the trail to the new capitol of Arkansas Territory in Little Rock. There we could take a river boat upstream to Cherokee lands and join another missionary there. Reverend Mason chose the safest route. A Baptist preacher on the White River, named George Gill, recommended it, and that was good enough for Jedidiah Mason.

* * *

When we finally reached Cherokee lands, I was eager to keep going. The Masons asked me to stay and live with them; I think they wanted me to marry Miss Sue, their oldest daughter. I spent the winter living with the Masons, meeting with Cherokees, and hearing of a possible war with the Osages, originally called the Wazhazhe. With the arrival of spring, I said my farewells and, with the blessing of Reverend Jedediah, started upstream to Fort Smith. Deep inside, I wanted to find, or find out, what happened to my father, and that answer lay farther to the west. Zebulon Pike in his exploration of the Southwest had mentioned conversations with an educated 'white man' (perhaps my father) living with Indians not far from a most unusual mountain (later called Pike's Peak). The story of Pike's journey was part of my education at Mr. Lisa's school in Saint Louis.

Across the Arkansas River from Fort Smith, I camped with a supply train heading upstream into Oklahoma Territory. They offered to let me join them if I would help with hunting and caring for the horses, an offer I did not refuse. I spent a couple of days with them as they got more supplies from Fort Smith and made a crossing with one of the supply boats just to see the Fort.

Staying on the north side of the river with the hunters, we traveled slowly by horseback on a trail probably made by Indians, narrow and winding. The supplies were on flat-bottomed boats being paddled upstream, sometimes towed. We were going to resupply an Army expedition in Colorado Territory. A few days into the journey we crossed into Oklahoma Territory, a soldier scout asked if I was interested in seeing a mystery, one he had discovered while stationed at Fort Smith. I had observed mounds on the south side of the river and thought perhaps he knew something of the source of the mounds. We were not making very good progress and could rejoin the supply train in a day's time.

On horseback, we traveled south beyond the mounds, to a place called Poteau Mountain by French trappers. Following a creek bed into the hills, the soldier showed me several giant stones with mysterious carvings in a language unfamiliar to me, or the scout. Sketching the markings in my journal, we rejoined the supply train. (*Years later I heard the markings were made by Vikings or other Nordic travelers, centuries earlier. The stones were called Rune Stones, probably meant to mark a claim of land, in a land that was unclaimed. The mounds we passed were later excavated and revealed an advanced Indian civilization living there several hundred years earlier, perhaps at the time of the Nordic travelers. It was indeed a mystery for me to ponder.)*

The course of the Arkansas River was familiar to the leader of the supply train, but confusing to me. In a week of travel, we had crossed two tributaries to the river that appeared equally large. At times, the river was wide and shallow, then narrowing into a deeper channel. After several weeks of travel, we camped near a Cheyenne Indian village in Colorado Territory and there I met several friendly Cheyenne.

During introductions, my name, Bellefleur, drew attention. They knew of a Frenchman with that name who met tribal hunters while hunting on the Platte River. He was following travelers on the Missouri River (Lewis and Clark) and had become separated from the group. According to the Indians, the Frenchman chose a squaw from their tribe and moved south with them toward the Arkansas River and their winter hunting grounds. He was well-liked by the tribe, but died on a buffalo hunt, in the path of a buffalo stampede. He was buried on the plains where he died, not far from where we were camped. A son of the Frenchman and Cheyenne squaw (my half-brother) was brought to meet me and led me to the place where he died. The son was given a Cheyenne name and was 13 winters old, his mother said he looked like our father, Jean Baptiste. A pile of stones marked his grave. *The Lewis and Clark Expedition camped near the Platte River looking to meet with prairie Indians on July 22, 1804, about the time of Bellefleur's defection, according to Mr. Clark.*

* * *

Our destination was about two days away. I continued with the supply train but made a map in my journal marking the place my father was buried. *The Bent brothers later (1833) built a fort near there to trade with the Cheyennes. Their historic fort still stands (reconstructed).* In the afternoon shadows of the Rocky Mountains along the swift-flowing Arkansas River, in the year 1824, I made a permanent camp, and set up shop as a boot maker using the cast iron lathe I had carried all the way from the Current River. (*As Paw might say, "Where the Arkansas River tumbles out of the Rocky Mountains onto the Eastern Plains of Colorado, I built my Council House!"*) My 'Quest' had ended, and I had found my father. Over the years I made several trips to visit the pile of stones on the prairie east of the Rocky Mountains. My Cheyenne brothers and sisters found a flowering plant that thrived in the desert plains and transplanted it as a remembrance. As years passed, I made boots for my schoolmate Jean Baptiste Charbonneau as he followed the Santa Fe Trail, traveling to the gold fields of California. He had a wandering spirit, but the friendship formed in Mr. Lisa's Saint Louis school became a bond we never forgot. I made moccasins for my Cheyenne relatives and friends from hides they brought me and softened with skillful hands.

When Reverend Jedediah Mason and his family came by on their journey to another mission field, this time in Oregon, I made shoes for the family as a gift. That, and the approaching winter season, prolonged their visit. Indians from my father's adopted tribe brought buffalo and elk skins for me to use in making moccasins, boots, and shoes. I should mention that while the Masons were staying in my "council house", I fell in love with their daughter, Miss Sue, now mature and most pleasing to the eye.

It is no coincidence Reverend Jedediah Mason married us that Spring alongside an Arkansas River village, just as he had performed the wedding of my parents in Shawnee Town, on the Ohio River. It was Sue who taught me how to tell Indians my name in sign language. Holding my two fists together, I tilt them apart, signing broken, or in my case Bro Ken. My Grandpa's wisdom passed to me, I leave with you – "all that live are your brothers and sisters!" I have had a good life and, by recording this adventure in a journal of many pages, my wish is someday a descendant will shed light on how we lived. We "did unto others as we would have them do unto us!"

An Epilogue

For the rest of the story, Pompey (Jean Baptiste Charbonneau) died in 1866 while traveling to a new gold field on the Oregon–Idaho border. (See photo above.) Reverend Jedediah Mason died in 1859, at the age of 99, in a Nez Perce missionary's home. Kentucky Baptiste Bellefleur (Bro Ken) died in the Arkansas River town called Pueblo at the ripe old age of 87, preceded in death by his wife, Sue Mason Bellefleur. He was survived by several children, including a son also named Kentucky, and called Ken. His boot lathe, bible, and journal were carried back to Chicago, Illinois by the adventurous son, Ken, in 1891, in time for the 1892 World's Columbian Exposition, celebrating Columbus' voyage 400 years earlier. Ken started a shoe shop in Illinois, a

German community with an Indian name, Mascoutah. He also had a son, born in Mascoutah, named Kenneth who learned to knap with flint.

Stones marking the grave of Jean Baptiste Bellefleur were later replaced with a marble slab inscribed "Our Father, Jean Baptiste".

As for the Obsidian Blade? It was passed on to Bro Ken's senior son who dropped the given name Kentucky to become just "plain old Ken". But plain old Ken learned something about the knife his forebearers never knew. In the hand of a blood descendant of the Nez Perce maiden, the coloring of the blade became more visible. When Ken took the blade with him to visit his maternal grandparents, the Masons in Nez Perce lands about 1855, the red shape in the blade began to glow brighter as he crossed the high-desert plains of Eastern Oregon. In the hand of a fellow traveler, the glow disappeared. The closer he got to "Glass Mountain" the brighter it glowed in Ken's hand. It was magical to watch.

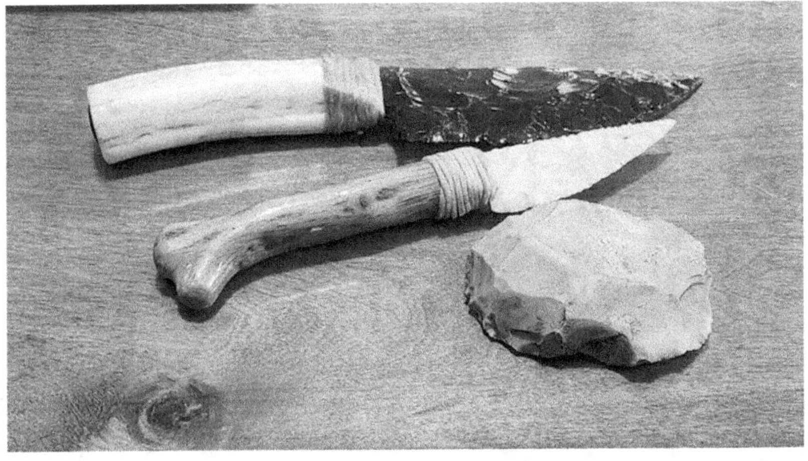

Photo of an Obsidian blade mounted in Elk antler, and a flint scraping tool.

* * *

In 1996, two Texas-born brothers, Ken, and Bob Brown, both now deceased, joined a church-building team from the Texas Hill Country traveling to Colorado to build a Baptist church on the Arkansas River above Pueblo. Ken was a retired Baptist Reverend called Bro-Ken by church members, and his wife's name, was Susan. The Arizona Baptist Builder they met in Colorado was named Ken Bellflower, a coincidence? Don Shadle, another Arizona Baptist Builder, and friend, does not think so! Another story to be told? And, if there is, who will tell the story? "What If?" is a collection of stories, first-person New Testament sermons by "Bro-Ken", Kenneth F. Brown, with a foreword by Chaplain Randy A. Marshal, USAF retired. There are more stories to be told!

A footnote to the story of Manuel Lisa, Kentucky's benefactor; Lisa died in 1820 from an illness picked up while traveling in the wilds of the Missouri River. John Jacob Astor brought his American Fur Company to Saint Louis two years later and made millions copying Lisa's system of remote forts, allowing trappers to swap their pelts for provisions. A radio reporter years later said this about Manuel Lisa, 'Other men took the title, "King of the Missouri," that Manuel Lisa truly deserved'.

--- 30 ---

The Rest of the Story

Researching the story of Walks With A Bear and Bro-Ken, led me to other stories, attached here to Bro Ken's story. They were copied from the internet and archives years ago. Credit for the stories that follow will eventually be discovered, and when that happens – thanks.

Pierre Gaultier de Varennes, sieur de La Vérendrye: Canadian Inland Explorer.

Pierre Gaultier de Varennes, sieur de La Vérendrye (1685-1749) was a Canadian soldier and explorer who traveled farther west than any previous European explorer had; he traveled to Winnipeg and then southwest, almost reaching the Missouri River. He was searching for a route across Canada from the Atlantic Ocean to the Pacific Ocean. His father was the sieur de Varennes, the governor of Trois Rivières, Quebec, Canada.

Born in Quebec, Canada, La Verendrye later fought in the War of Spanish Succession (1699-1713). He went to Europe where he fought at the battle of Malplaquet (1708) and was badly wounded. After returning to Canada, he became a fur trader and farmer. His brother was given the fur trade rights to a vast area of land north of Lake Superior in 1726, and Pierre joined him in this business. Pierre decided to search for a route across Canada (believing that Canada was much smaller than it actually was). After talking to Native Americans in what is now Thunder Bay, Ontario, he thought he might be able to reach the Pacific Ocean via the Saskatchewan River. In 1730, the government of Quebec funded La Verendrye's proposed expedition across Canada. He left Montreal on June 8, 1731, with three of his sons and others. They built forts at Rainy Lake and at Lake of the Woods and eventually reached Lake Winnipeg, but there were fights with the Sioux Indians in 1736, in which many members of the expedition died, including one of La Verendrye's sons (Jean Baptiste).

La Verendrye continued to search for the Saskatchewan River and the Mandan Indians, who were thought to live on the Saskatchewan River and perhaps know a route to the Pacific Ocean. From Lake Winnipeg, he and his two other sons (Louis Joseph and François) traveled southwest in 1738, where the Mandans lived (on the Missouri River though, not the Saskatchewan River as La Verendrye thought). They returned to the fort at Lake of the Woods in 1739. Returning to Quebec in 1744, he died December 5, 1749, while planning another expedition in search of the Saskatchewan River. His sons continued to explore Canada.

* * *

More About the Verendryes

Pierre Gaultier de Varennes, Sieur de La Verendrye, was born in New France (in Canada) on Nov. 17, 1685, at Three Rivers (Trois-Riviéres) trading post in Quebec. In his early teens, Verendrye joined the French Colonial army, fighting the English and Indians in New England and Newfoundland and later serving in Flanders during the War of the Spanish Succession.

Upon his return to Three Rivers, he married Marie-Anne Dandonneau, in 1712. The couple had six children, including four sons – two of whom would later explore the Dakotas on their own. Verendrye soon became a fur trader, serving from 1726 to 1731 as commandant of a chain of fur posts. Indians visiting the posts often spoke of a great river flowing to the Western Ocean. They also told stories of the mysterious Mandans, "white Indians" living in what is now North Dakota, whose dwellings resembled those of the French. Such stories fired Verendrye's imagination, and he was determined to hunt for the river to the sea, as well as the fabled "white Indians."

He devised a plan to do both. In 1728 and 1729, Verendrye sought and won approval for his project from the governments in Quebec and France. Financing for the venture came from Montreal merchants eager to cash in on furs from newly discovered territory.

* * *

The Journeys Begin

In 1731, Verendrye, three of his sons, and around 50 voyageurs set out by canoe traveling to the northern boundary waters of Minnesota. There, he established a chain of trading posts from Lake of the Woods (where his oldest son was later killed by Indians) to Lake Winnipeg. Verendrye's supporters were upset when he returned to Quebec in 1734 without having discovered the western waterway. In June of 1735, Verendrye set out again, determined to find the waterway to the Pacific Ocean, and the Mandan Indians. Along the way, he and his men built several posts near present-day Winnipeg, including Fort La Reine.

In November of 1738, Verendrye and a party of 52 (including his remaining sons) began their epic journey from Fort La Reine. Hundreds of Assiniboines joined them as escorts. The party reached present-day North Dakota, traveling a circuitous route past the Pembina and Turtle mountains, then southwest along the Souris River. On the evening of the 28th, they encountered their first Mandans and were invited to their village. Verendrye soon discovered the stories of the "white Indians" had been greatly exaggerated – although he did describe the Mandans thus in his journals: "This nation is mixed white and black ... many with blonde and fair hair." Verendrye's writings provide the earliest records of the Mandans.

Although the weather was bitter and their Mandan hosts gracious and accommodating, Verendrye decided to head home in midwinter. Battling a brutal illness, he departed with his companions on Jan. 13, arriving at Fort La Reine on Feb. 11, 1739, "still greatly fatigued and very ill," he wrote. Upon his return to New France, Verendrye received no hero's welcome. Instead, deep in debt, he was denounced for failing in his mission of discovering the Pacific water route.

Five years after his voyage, however, Verendrye's contributions to exploration and industry were recognized by the King of France via the prestigious Croix de Saint-Louis award. He was also assigned to manage the western fur posts. Verendrye died in Montreal on Dec. 6, 1749, before he could reach his goal of finding the westward-flowing river leading to the Pacific Ocean.

A remarkable find. In 1742, two of Verendrye's sons, Louis Joseph and Francois, continued their father's quest for a western waterway. They left Fort La Reine for the Mandan villages, following the Mouse River past the present town of Verendrye to the Missouri River. Guided by Indians they met on the way, the Verendryes traveled for 21 days, south and west. On Jan. 1, 1743, the brothers reported seeing snow-capped mountains – possibly the Big Horn Mountains in Wyoming, or perhaps the Black Hills. Returning to the Missouri River, the Verendryes stopped near Fort Pierre, S.D. There, on March 30, 1743, on a high promontory overlooking the river, they buried an engraved lead plate attesting to their voyage.

On Feb. 16, 1913, on a hill overlooking Fort Pierre, S.D., some school children discovered a curious lead plate, half buried in the earth. That plate, planted by the Verendrye brothers 170 years earlier, now rests in the South Dakota State Archives' Cultural Heritage Center in Pierre, S.D.

* * *

A Link to The Lewis and Clark Expedition

Spending several sleepless nights as they proceeded through the lands occupied by the powerful "Teton" Lakota tribes. The captains had been warned that these tribes exacted a high toll before allowing any traffic on the river to pass and that if the price they named was not met, the Lakota would take it by force. The journal entries for the dates of September 23–30 note that the soldiers were on high alert during their stay in the vicinity of present-day Pierre and Fort Pierre.

The captains' worst fears were almost realized during their first meeting with the local Lakota chiefs at the mouth of the Bad (Teton) River. The lack of a competent interpreter sent the council to the brink of violence with weapons drawn and sighted on both sides. Given the time it took to reload the guns carried by the army volunteers, the advantage lay on the side of the Lakota warriors, whose bows could be re-nocked with greater speed. The "Teton" Chief, Black Buffalo, managed to diffuse the situation, gaining him greater status with his own people, and with the Army officers.

Although Lewis & Clark spent the next few days talking to, lecturing, feasting with, and studying the Lakota people, the tension didn't ease. In fact, it almost erupted into violence a second time. Sometime after 1 a.m., after a night of feasting and being entertained by Native dancers, Clark boarded a pirogue bound for the keelboat. The steersman inadvertently ran over the anchor cable of the keelboat, sending the vessel to the mercy of the current. The shouting of men trying to regain control of the keelboat alarmed the "Teton" warriors who lined the riverbanks apparently prepared for battle.

The next day brought the final "battle of wills" and violence between the Expedition and the Lakota was narrowly avoided for a third time. Followers of Chief Black Buffalo grabbed the rope tethering the keelboat to the riverbank and wouldn't release it, demanding more tobacco. Lewis refused. Tempers flared on both sides as armed warriors again lined the bank, and Clark prepared to fire the port swivel gun. Lewis insisted that the Corps would proceed, and calling Black Buffalo's leadership into question, goaded the Chief into significantly reducing the amount the warriors were demanding. This done, Lewis disdainfully tossed a few twists of tobacco toward the men holding onto the rope, and Black Buffalo jerking the rope from their hands, handed it to the steersman. The encounter with the "Tetons" was over.

Today, you can stand in the grass in a city-owned park at the mouth of the Bad River and envision the keelboat anchored 70 yards out in the middle of the Missouri River. Imagine yourself surrounded by proud Lakota warriors watching the US soldiers parade in full military dress. Or, you can drive a little north of town and overlook the approximate area where the anchor was lost. And, so concludes your history lesson for the day. Joe Hipp

www.ingramcontent.com/pod-product-compliance
Lightning Source LLC
Chambersburg PA
CBHW061645130726
47996CB00003B/1463